DR. TENMA

ALLIANCE: Darkness and ambition
Astro's creator who now plots to rule the
world with Robots.
ROBOTS WILL RULE!

HARLEY

ALLIANCE: Omega Nights
The world's best rocket ball player, Harley is loved
by his fans.
GO TEAM!

Astro Boy: Rocket Ball
Copyright © 2005 Tezuka Productions/Sony Pictures Entertainment (Japan) Inc.
ASTRO BOY character:™ & © 2005 Tezuka productions.
All rights reserved. Distributed by Sony Pictures Television.

1 3 5 7 9 8 6 4 2
0-00-720016-1

First published in Great Britain in 2005 by HarperCollins *Children's Books*
HarperCollins *Children's Books* is an imprint of HarperCollins Publishers Ltd
77-85 Fulham Palace Road, Hammersmith, London W6 8JB.

Printed and bound in China.

www.harpercollinschildrensbooks.co.uk
www.astroboytv.com

ASTRO BOY®
ROCKET BALL

By Acton Figueroa

Based on the teleplay by Stan Berkowitz

HarperCollins *Children's Books*

Astro and Dr. O'Shay were riding in their air-car high above Metro City. Astro looked down, far below.

"What's going on down there?" he asked.

"That's the Rocket Ball Championship," said Dr. O'Shay.

That sounded like fun to Astro. "I'm going to play, too!" he shouted. Astro zoomed down to the ground, using his jet rockets.

Astro flew right into the middle of the robots playing in the Rocket Ball Championship. They were very big robots. Harley, the best player of all, was running down the field.

Astro didn't know the rules, so he caught the ball. The referee didn't like this. Astro would need to learn the rules!

The next day, Astro's visit to the Rocket Ball Championship was in all the newspapers. One person was very interested – Dr. Tenma, the man who created Astro. After he built Astro, Dr. Tenma had set fire to his lab, abandoned the robot and gone into hiding. Now that Dr. Tenma knew where Astro was, he wanted to keep watch over Astro.

In the park, Nicholas and his friend were teaching
Astro how to play rocket ball and follow the rules.

A robot-dog named Cerebus interrupted their game.
It took their ball and ran off. Astro and Nicholas followed it.
The dog ran and ran until it came to the stadium where
the Rocket Ball Championship was still being played. The
robot-dog used its lasers to cut open the fence. It ran right
into the stadium, and Astro and his friend Nicholas followed.

Dr. O'Shay was worried. He couldn't find Astro anywhere. But Dr. Tenma knew where Astro was. It was Dr. Tenma's robot-dog that led Astro to the stadium. Dr. Tenma wanted to test Astro.

On the playing field, something
strange was going on. Harley usually
played fairly. Today he wasn't playing
fair at all. He wasn't following the rules.

Dr. Tenma was controlling Harley.
It was all part of his plan.

Dr. O'Shay tracked Astro on his air-car computer and jetted down to the rocket ball stadium. Just as he landed, the doors and windows and even the roof of the stadium began sliding shut. Dr. Tenma had closed off every exit. Everyone inside was trapped!

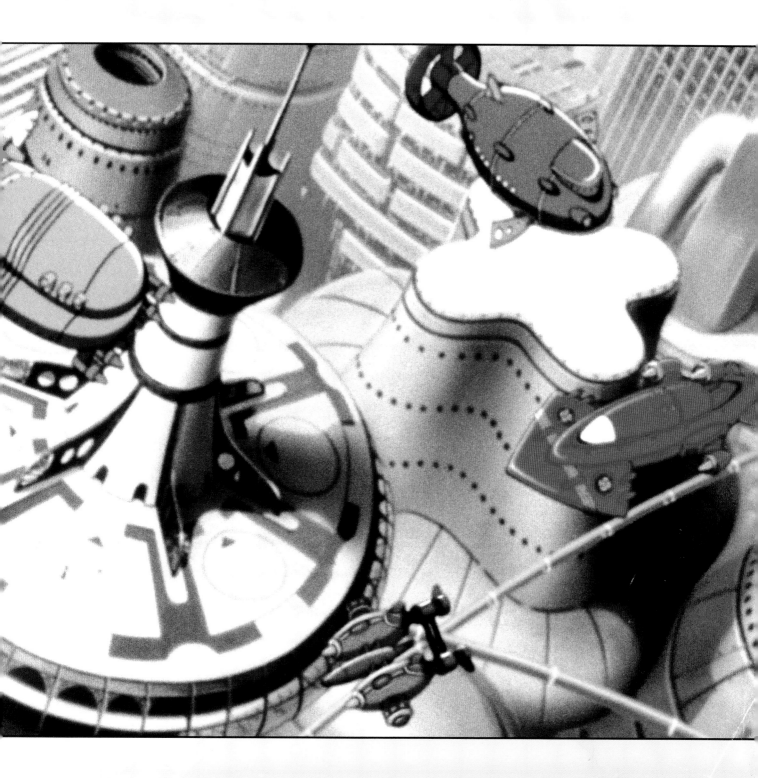

Dr. Tenma used his robot-dog, Cerebus, to challenge Astro to a game against Harley and Team Omega.

Astro didn't ask what would happen if he lost. Dr. Tenma was a very bad guy. If Astro didn't do what he wanted, something terrible would happen to the people in the stadium.

Harley stood on the playing field waiting for Astro. The people in the stands were quiet. They were afraid. What would Astro do?

Dr. O'Shay had been watching Harley play. He had heard Dr. Tenma's challenge to Astro. He knew something was wrong, and he knew he had to help Astro. He ran to the announcer's room in the stadium and logged on to their computer. He had to find out why Harley had turned into a bad robot.

Astro was ready to play. As he stood before Harley, he looked around at the people in the stands. He had to win this game. He had to save the fans.

"I'll play a match with Harley," said Astro, "but I'll play fair!"

Astro swooped around the field. Harley was the best
rocket ball player ever, but Astro was on a mission.

Astro scored! The crowd cheered!

Harley wouldn't give up. He transformed with his teammates into the biggest robot ever.

High up in the stadium, Dr. O'Shay had found out how Dr. Tenma was controlling Harley. "His sunglasses, Astro!" he yelled. "Take his sunglasses!"

Astro used his last bit of strength to dodge the giant robot. He flew up to Harley's face and grabbed the sunglasses. The giant robot collapsed. The crowd was quiet. The people watched. Would the good Harley come back?

Harley said, "Sorry, but you are only allowed on the field if you know the rules!" He wanted to make sure everyone was safe. Yes! The old Harley was back – fair-play Harley! Astro had saved the crowd in the stadium and their favourite robot player, too.

As Astro left the stadium, the crowd cheered for him. "Astro! Astro! Astro!"

What a good day!

ASTRO

ALLIANCE: Robots and humans
Astro is a jet powered robot with a
heart of gold. He believes in both human
and robot rights.
ROBOTS AND HUMANS UNITE!

DR. O'SHAY

ALLIANCE: Robots and humans
Dr. O'Shay heads the ministry of Science
and is like a father to Astro.
ROBOTS HAVE FEELINGS TOO!

DR. TENMA

ALLIANCE: Darkness and ambition
Astro's creator who now plots to rule the
world with Robots.
ROBOTS WILL RULE!

HARLEY

ALLIANCE: Omega Nights
The world's best rocket ball player, Harley is loved
by his fans.
GO TEAM!